Nate the Great
and The
Hungry
Book
Club

Nate the Great
and The
Hungry
Book
Club

by Marjorie Weinman Sharmat
and Mitchell Sharmat

illustrated by Jody Wheeler
in the style of Marc Simont

A Yearling Book

We want to thank the members of the Harvard Book Club of Southern Arizona for the inspiration they innocently and inadvertently provided for this book. —Marjorie Weinman Sharmat and Mitchell Sharmat

This is a work of fiction. Names, characters, places, and incidents either are the product of the author's imagination or are used fictitiously. Any resemblance to actual persons, living or dead, events, or locales is entirely coincidental.

Text copyright © 2009 by Marjorie Weinman Sharmat and Mitchell Sharmat
New illustrations of Nate the Great, Sludge, Rosamond, Annie, Oliver, Pip, Finley, Claude, Esmeralda, Harry, Fang, and the Hexes by Jody Wheeler based upon the original drawings by Marc Simont. All other images copyright © 2009 by Jody Wheeler
Cover art copyright © 2009 by Jody Wheeler
Extra Fun Activities copyright © 2011 by Emily Costello
Extra Fun Activities illustrations copyright © 2011 by Jody Wheeler

All rights reserved. Published in the United States by Yearling, an imprint of Random House Children's Books, a division of Random House, Inc., New York. Originally published in hardcover in the United States by Delacorte Press, an imprint of Random House Children's Books, New York, in 2009.

Yearling and the jumping horse design are registered trademarks of Random House, Inc.

Visit us on the Web! www.randomhouse.com/kids
Educators and librarians, for a variety of teaching tools, visit us at www.randomhouse.com/teachers

The Library of Congress has cataloged the hardcover edition of this work as follows:
Sharmat, Marjorie Weinman.
Nate the Great and the hungry book club / by Marjorie Weinman Sharmat and Mitchell Sharmat; illustrated by Jody Wheeler in the style of Marc Simont. — 1st ed.
p. cm.
Summary: Nate and his dog Sludge help Rosamond discover who has been tearing pages out of her books.
ISBN 978-0-385-73695-4 (trade hc : alk. paper) — ISBN 978-0-385-90637-1 (glb : alk. paper)
[1. Mystery and detective stories. 2. Books and reading—Fiction.] I. Sharmat, Mitchell.
II. Wheeler, Jody, ill. III. Title.
PZ7.S5299 Natp 2009
[Fic]—dc22
2009030319

ISBN 978-0-375-84548-2 (pbk.)
Printed in the United States of America
15 14 13 12 11 10 9
First Yearling Edition 2011

Chapter One
Torn, Ripped, Ruined

My name is Nate the Great.
I am a detective.
My dog, Sludge, is a detective too.
"Ouch!"
Right now I am a mumbling, bumbling,
tripping detective.
I have just tripped over
a big pile of books
that Rosamond left in my house.

Sludge is sniffing them.

He has been sniffing them

since Rosamond knocked on my door

this morning.

She was carrying a bunch of books.

Three more were piled on her head.

Rosamond looked very strange.

Rosamond looks strange all the time.

"I have great news," she said.

"I have started a book club.

I am calling it Rosamond's Ready Readers.

But there is trouble in the club.

One of the members is trying

to wreck my cookbook. Look!"

Rosamond took a book off her head.

The other two books fell off.

"Why are you carrying books on top

of your head?" I asked.

"Because I'm president of a club now.

These books help me hold my head high
and look like a president."
I, Nate the Great, knew that I was
looking at a very strange president.

"This is my new cookbook," she said.
"Yesterday I left it open on my
kitchen table after I made treats
for the club meeting.
When the meeting was over,
I went to get the treats
for the members.
The page that was open
was torn, ripped, *ruined*!"
Sludge and I looked at the page.
I, Nate the Great, say that
it was torn, ripped, ruined.

Chapter Two
The Crime Scene

Rosamond pulled something out of
her pocket.

"Here is a photo of the crime scene,"
she said.

I looked at the photo. "Your kitchen
was a crime scene?"

"Of course. Keep this photo and study it.
You can see that my cookbook
is in the middle of my huge, high table.

The torn page had a recipe for tuna fish pie.
The bits of pie that fell
on the page are gone too.
I want you to find the evil monster
who did this!"

"Monster?"

"Yes. The Evil Page Monster,"
Rosamond said.

"Now, here is my plan. The next meeting
will be at my house this afternoon.
You and Sludge can come undercover.
Just pretend you are new members.
I'll be using this cookbook again.
Meanwhile, I'll leave these other
books here, where they'll be safe.
I left one book at home.
The members will be reading it
at today's meeting."
Rosamond piled her books on my floor.
"You are so lucky to have this case!"

I, Nate the Great, did not agree.

"Perhaps this is a case for a bookworm,"
I said.

"Enjoy being a bookworm," Rosamond said.

I looked at Sludge.

We both knew that if I didn't take the case,
Rosamond would come back.

And back. And back.

And back.

Chapter Three
A Book Case

I wrote a note to my mother.

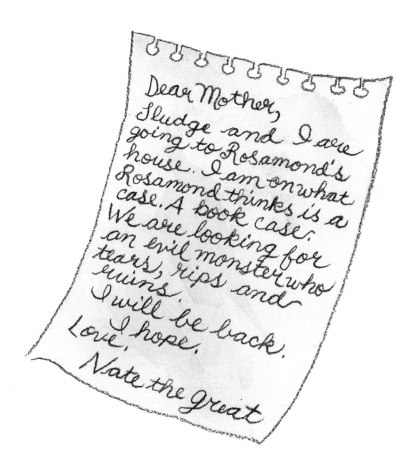

Dear Mother,
Sludge and I are going to Rosamond's house. I am on what Rosamond thinks is a case. A book case. We are looking for an evil monster who tears, rips and ruins.
I will be back, I hope.
Love,
Nate the Great

Chapter Four
The Hungry Book Club

It was afternoon.

Sludge and I went to Rosamond's house.

She answered the door.

She had only one book on her head.

I peered inside her house.

I saw Oliver, Pip, Finley, Claude,
Esmeralda, Annie, and Annie's little
brother, Harry, sitting in a circle.

Also sitting in the circle were Annie's
dog, Fang, and Rosamond's four cats,
Plain Hex, Little Hex, Big Hex,
and Super Hex.

I stepped back. "The Hexes and Fang
belong to your book club?"
"Sure," Rosamond said.
"Everybody loves stories.
And treats. I serve tuna fish pie to the
cats and meat patties to Fang.
Everybody else gets cookies.

This is a very hungry book club.
Come in."
"I, Nate the Great, am not in the mood
for cookies or circles," I said.
"Sludge and I will sit in a corner."

Chapter Five
Meet Harvard Hedgehog

Rosamond sat down in a big chair.
She took the book off her head.
She held it up.
"This is our book for today,"
she announced.
"*Harvard Hedgehog*.
We will take turns reading it out loud.
Then we will talk about the book.
I will start.

'Harvard Hedgehog was always late.
He arrived at parties just in time
to bump into everyone leaving.
He nibbled leftover cake crumbs
and lapped melted ice cream.
Then he sat in a corner
and exclaimed, "Wonderful party!"
to the empty room.'"

I, Nate the Great, was sitting in a corner
like Harvard Hedgehog.
I pretended to go to sleep.
But I was watching, watching.
The book went from member to member.
Nobody was tearing pages.
It was Esmeralda's turn to read.

"'When Harvard went to the movies,
he always got there
when the movie was over.
As everyone was going out,
Harvard was going in.
He would sit down on stale popcorn
and look up at the big, empty screen.
"Great show!" he exclaimed to no one.
Harvard meant to be on time,
but he never was. . . .'"

Suddenly Esmeralda stopped reading.
She looked puzzled.
"A page is missing," she said.
Rosamond looked straight at me.
"A ripped page in one book
and now a missing page from another.
When I bought this book,
there were no pages missing.
I know because I read the entire book
before I bought it!"
I, Nate the Great, looked at Sludge.
I now knew we had a real case.

Chapter Six
Double Trouble

Rosamond raised her arms.
"As president of Rosamond's Ready
Readers, I will not let this stop
our book club meeting.
Members, who would like to tell me
what you think of the book so far?"
Esmeralda raised her hand. "At first I
thought that Harvard needed a watch,
but now I know he needs a page."

Claude raised his hand.
Claude was always losing things.
"I don't like the book
because Harvard doesn't lose anything,"
he said. "If you never lose anything,
you never have a chance to find
what you didn't lose."
"Excellent thought," Rosamond said.

Oliver spoke up. "I follow people.
Everyone knows I do.
Harvard doesn't
follow anybody. Harvard is
a very boring hedgehog."

"Thank you for sharing that with us,"
Rosamond said.

"Me, me, me!" Harry was
jumping up and down.
"I like the book.
I like the picture of
Harvard smiling in front of
the big clock the best."

Rosamond smiled.
"Well, we have a nice happy Harvard,
and a happy Harry," she said.

"I am proud of all my members.
Except whoever ripped a page
and took a page."

I, Nate the Great, was thinking.
Who would rip
a page of the cookbook and
take a page of *Harvard Hedgehog*?
Someone who liked the books,
or someone who disliked the books?
Or someone who couldn't decide?
And where was the missing page?
"I would like to see the book," I said.

Rosamond handed it to me.

"I see that the missing page
would have been numbered 15 on one side
and 16 on the other," I said.

"Numbers, crumbers," Rosamond said.

"You have a double mystery.
Just solve it!"

Chapter Seven
The Evil Page Monster

Rosamond stood up.
"Now it's time for treats," she said.
"The animals are getting restless."
Sludge and I followed Rosamond
to the kitchen.
It was a mess.
But Sludge sniffed and sniffed.
He liked this case
because it smelled good.
I saw a cookbook on the table.

This time the book was open
to a recipe for meat patties.
There were bits of meat on the page.
Rosamond must have been using the
cookbook today to make her treats.
This page had no rips.
Hmmm.

Fang and the Hexes walked in.
Fang sniffed the table.
He started to jump up
and reach for the cookbook.
"Stop!" Rosamond yelled.
"You, Fang, are the Evil Page Monster!

I, President Rosamond,
have solved this case.
Fang must have sneaked in
during yesterday's meeting,
eaten the bits of food,
and ripped the page.
And now I've stopped him
from doing it again."
Rosamond folded her arms
and looked at me.
"Time to find the missing page," she said.
I, Nate the Great, had two choices.
I could search for the missing page
or I could go home and eat pancakes
and think.

Chapter Eight
Sniffs

I ate my pancakes
while Sludge ate a bone.
Then Sludge walked around the room.
He was looking for something.
And he found it.
It was the photo Rosamond had left here.
He sniffed it and sniffed it and sniffed it.
Was he trying to tell me something?

Was the ripped-page case really solved?
Did Fang really do it?
I looked at the photo again.
The page in the cookbook
had no food on it.
The page I had seen at Rosamond's house
had tiny bits of meat on it.

The recipe in the photo was for
tuna fish pie.
The recipe at her house was for
meat patties.
One recipe for cats, one recipe for dogs.
"Good work, Sludge," I said.

Chapter Nine
Not So Fast

I called Rosamond.
"I am coming back to your house," I said.
"And I need Annie and Fang to be there."
I put the photo of the tuna fish pie page
in my pocket.

Sludge and I rushed to Rosamond's house.
Rosamond was waiting for us at the door.
"Your ripped-page case is not solved,"
I said.

"That fangy Fang did it!" Rosamond said.
"And here he comes down the street
with Annie."
"We must all go into the kitchen," I said.
Rosamond, Annie, Fang, Sludge, and I
went into the kitchen.
The cookbook was still open on the table.
Fang sniffed and ran to the table.
"Ho hum," Rosamond said. "We already
know that Fang ripped a page yesterday."

"Wait!" I said.

Fang jumped up and put his front paws
on the table.

He opened his jaws.

He stretched.

But he couldn't reach the cookbook.

"This table is too high and big for Fang,"
I said.

"Poor Fang," Annie said. "He's big
and smart, but he isn't that stretchy."

I, Nate the Great, already knew that.
Fang would have grabbed the bits of meat
during the meeting
if he could have reached them!
Rosamond sighed. "Okay, so Fang
couldn't have ripped the page yesterday."
"Correct," I said. "Also, he doesn't
like tuna fish pie."
I pulled the cookbook photo out of
my pocket.

"This photo shows the cookbook open
to a tuna fish pie recipe. But the open
pages have no bits of tuna fish on them."
"I already knew that," Rosamond said.
"I, Nate the Great, say that someone
reached for those tuna fish bits
and was scratching and tearing
to get every last bite."
"Who?" Rosamond asked.

"Little Hex," I said. "He can leap high.
Also, he can hide in small spaces.
He is so small that he could have
gone into the kitchen and come back
without your seeing him."
Rosamond clapped her hands.
"Little Hex is growing up!
My darling little Page Monster."
"I, Nate the Great, say that
the ripped-page case is solved.
And you should try to keep your
kitchen neater.
Clean clues are better."
I took two bones from my pocket
and gave one to Fang and one to Sludge.
Rosamond kept clapping.
"Little Hex must have taken the
Harvard Hedgehog page too.
What a talent he has!"
"Not so fast," I said.

"You are trying to reuse a clue.
Little Hex might not have taken
the page.
Tell me everything about
your *Harvard Hedgehog* book."
"Well, yesterday Annie and I went to the
book sale at the school around the corner.
I bought the book there.
I read it before I bought it.
There weren't any missing pages.
After I bought the book,
I kept it with me.
In my hands. On my head.

I even slept with it."
"Is there anything else
I should know?" I asked.
"No. I'm a president. I think
of everything."
"Then I must leave," I said.
"Leave? But you just came."
"That's how it is
in the detective business," I said.
"We come. We go.
We go where the clues take us."
I, Nate the Great, knew that
I needed more clues.
If the book was with Rosamond
all the time,
how could a page be missing?

BOOK SALE
TODAY
9-5

Chapter Ten
Stretchy Fang

Annie, Fang, Sludge, and I left
Rosamond's house.
"I am looking for a new clue,"
I said to Annie. "A missing-page clue."
"I don't have any clue," Annie said.
"But I want you to know
that Fang can be stretchy
some of the time. You should have
seen him at the school book sale."

"What?" I said. "He was there?"
"I brought him along when
I went with Rosamond," Annie said.
"Tell me exactly how
Fang was stretchy there," I said.
"Well, we went to the Used Books table.
A lady there told us that some books
might have food stains,
loose bindings, and faded pages.
Rosamond began picking through books
and reading them.
If she liked a book, she put it in a pile
on the table.
Suddenly Fang put his paws on the table
and started to sniff a book.
There were stains on it
that looked like
chicken noodle soup.
Fang licked the book.

Then he pawed through
more books and licked pages.
Lots of books fell to the floor.
Fang was really stretchy.
It was his kind of table."

"Then what happened?"
"I picked up the books that
Fang had licked and I bought them.
Rosamond's pile had toppled over,
but she scooped up her books
from the table and the floor
and bought them.

We both went home with full bags.
Since Fang had licked and liked the
books, I put them all in his doghouse."
"Thank you for the information," I said.
I turned to Sludge.
"You and I are going to school!"

Chapter Eleven
School Clues

Sludge and I rushed to the school.

The book sale was in the gym.

A lady walked up to us.

I knew she was a librarian because
she had a badge on her shirt that said
LIBRARIAN.

Sometimes being a detective is easy.

"Hello," I said. "I am looking for
Harvard Hedgehog."
"You're in luck," the librarian said.
"We've sold two copies of *Harvard*,
but we still have one left.
And here he is on the table."
"Do you have pages 15 and 16?" I asked.
"Yes. The pages are in good shape.
Clean, and with strong binding."

"No chicken noodle soup?" I said.

"What?"

"I was just thinking.

I'm a detective.

I think a lot.

I think I will buy this book."

I bought the book and thanked
the librarian.

Then Sludge and I went home.

Chapter Twelve
The Hedgehog Picture

I sat down in my favorite chair.
I opened my *Harvard Hedgehog* book.
I turned to page 15.
There was a picture of Harvard
getting his photo taken
in front of a big clock.

He looked proud. And he was smiling.
But why would anyone take *that* page?
I, Nate the Great, say that
there must be far better things
in this world to watch
than a hedgehog posing for his photo.
And then I remembered something.
What I had just seen
in the book was not news to me.
I had already heard about it.
I, Nate the Great, was about
to solve this case.

Chapter Thirteen
Reading Together

I had two clues.
School clues.
I was told that the pages
in my book were in good shape.
Clean. Strong binding.
Annie was told that some books
had loose bindings.
Hmmm. Pages. Bindings.

I, Nate the Great, say that a loose binding
could cause a loose page,
and a loose page could become
a missing page.
There had been three copies of the
Harvard Hedgehog book at the
Used Books table.

Rosamond had picked a good copy.
But when her pile fell down,
she must have grabbed the copy
that had the missing page.
She didn't know it.
Annie must have bought the good copy
that Rosamond had picked out,
and she didn't know it.

And how did I, Nate the Great, know it?
Because I now remembered where I had
heard about Harvard Hedgehog smiling in
front of a big clock.
From Harry! At the book club meeting.
But how could Harry have known
what was on page 15, since it was missing?
Because he had seen the book at home!
Harry must have been looking
at Fang's books.
And he saw the Harvard Hedgehog picture.

I turned to Sludge.

"I must give this book to Rosamond
and tell her that the case is solved.
I must also tell Annie to feed Fang
plenty of chicken noodle soup.

But there is something else
I want to do first."
I, Nate the Great, picked up every book
that Rosamond had brought over
and carefully put them on a shelf.
"Just where they should be," I said.

Then I took my *Harvard Hedgehog* book
and sat down in my chair.
"I am going to read this book
as a reader and not
as a detective," I said.
"Let's read it together."
Sludge jumped up on my lap.
And I, Nate the Great, read and read
until I reached . . .

~Extra~
Fun Activities!

What's Inside

Nate went to the library. He found a book about hedgehogs. It was the kind of book with facts in it. Here's what he learned.

NATE'S NOTES: Hedgehogs

Hedgehogs are animals about the size of a guinea pig. They like to root around in hedges. They're not searching for clues. They're searching for food! They make a hog-like snort while they search. That's how they got their name! Hedge + hog = hedgehog.

Don't look for wild hedgehogs in the United States. They live in Africa, Britain, and Asia.

About five thousand short, prickly spines cover a hedgehog's back. These spines are called quills. Quills are hollow shafts like the shafts of bird feathers. They aren't poisonous or barbed. Still, they are weapons. If you get poked with one, it hurts!

When they're scared, hedgehogs roll into a tight ball. Their quills protect their face, eyes, arms, legs, and bellies. Pet hedgehogs usually weigh less than a pound. Wild ones get a little bigger.

In the wild, hedgehogs live by themselves.
They are nocturnal. That means they
sleep during the day. They eat and play
at night. Hedgehogs can't see very well,
but they have a great sense of smell.

Like bears, hedgehogs hibernate during
winter. That means they go to sleep for
days on end. On warm days, hedgehogs
may wake up to eat and drink. But mostly
they sleep in burrows or piles of leaves
until spring.

Hedgehogs:
• purr when they
are happy.

• squeal when they
are frightened.

• grunt like pigs when
they are looking for
tasty food.

A baby hedgehog is called a hoglet.

Hedgehogs like to eat slugs, earthworms, moths, and other bugs. They steal eggs from ground-nesting birds' nests and gobble them down.

Hedgehogs sometimes twist their head around and spit on their quills! Then they spread the spit around with their tongues. Nobody knows why they do this. Some scientists say it happens when they sniff a good-smelling frog or worm. Maybe they are fighting off ticks. Nate thinks it's too gross to think about much.

Some people keep hedgehogs as pets. Hedgehog quills lie flat unless the animal feels threatened. A human who develops a trusting relationship with a hedgehog can pet it from its face to its back. Some hedgehogs will also cuddle in people's hands or laps. Of course, there are hedgehogs who don't like to cuddle, just like there are people who prefer to be left alone.

Pet hedgehogs eat cat food.

Funny Pages

Q: What happened when Sludge wrote the story of his life?

A: *It got on the best smellers' list.*

Q: Why did the librarian slip and fall?

A: *She was in the non-friction section.*

Q: Why was the T. rex afraid to go to the library?
A: *Because his books were 60 million years overdue.*

Q: Why didn't the book club like the
phone book?
A: *It had too many characters.*

Q: What did the librarian hang over her
baby's crib?
A: *A book mobile.*

Q: Why does the elephant use his trunk as a
   bookmark?
A: *That way he nose where he stopped reading.*

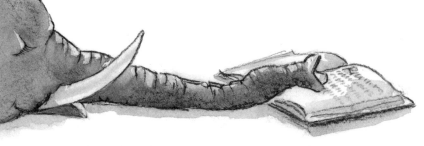

Q: What did the mummy do at the library?
A: *Got wrapped up in a good mystery.*

Q: Why are frogs librarians' favorite animals?
A: *Because frogs say "Rrredit, rrredit, rrredit."*

Have you helped solve all
Nate the Great's mysteries?

❑ **Nate the Great:** Meet Nate, the great detective, and join him as he uses incredible sleuthing skills to solve his first big case.

❑ **Nate the Great Goes Undercover:** Who— or what—is raiding Oliver's trash every night? Nate bravely hides out in his friend's garbage can to catch the smelly crook.

❑ **Nate the Great and the Lost List:** Nate loves pancakes, but who ever heard of cats eating them? Is a strange recipe at the heart of this mystery?

❑ **Nate the Great and the Phony Clue:** Against ferocious cats, hostile adversaries, and a sly phony clue, Nate struggles to prove that he's still the world's greatest detective.

❑ **Nate the Great and the Sticky Case:** Nate is stuck with his stickiest case yet as he hunts for his friend Claude's valuable stegosaurus stamp.

❑ **Nate the Great and the Missing Key:** Nate isn't afraid to look anywhere—even under the nose of his friend's ferocious dog, Fang—to solve the case of the missing key.

- **Nate the Great and the Snowy Trail:** Nate has his work cut out for him when his friend Rosamond loses the birthday present she was going to give him. How can he find the present when Rosamond won't even tell him what it is?

- **Nate the Great and the Fishy Prize:** The trophy for the Smartest Pet Contest has disappeared! Will Sludge, Nate's clue-sniffing dog, help solve the case and prove he's worthy of the prize?

- **Nate the Great Stalks Stupidweed:** When his friend Oliver loses his special plant, Nate searches high and low. Who knew a little weed could be so tricky?

- **Nate the Great and the Boring Beach Bag:** It's no relaxing day at the beach for Nate and his trusty dog, Sludge, as they search through sand and surf for signs of a missing beach bag.

- **Nate the Great Goes Down in the Dumps:** Nate discovers that the only way to clean up this case is to visit the town dump. Detective work can sure get dirty!

- **Nate the Great and the Halloween Hunt:** It's Halloween, but Nate isn't trick-or-treating for candy. Can any of the witches, pirates, and robots he meets help him find a missing cat?

- **Nate the Great and the Musical Note:** Nate is used to looking for clues, not listening for them! When he gets caught in the middle of a musical riddle, can he hear his way out?

- **Nate the Great and the Stolen Base:** It's not easy to track down a stolen base, and Nate's hunt leads him to some strange places before he finds himself at bat once more.

- **Nate the Great and the Pillowcase:** When a pillowcase goes missing, Nate must venture into the dead of night to search for clues. Everyone sleeps easier knowing Nate the Great is on the case!

- **Nate the Great and the Mushy Valentine:** Nate hates mushy stuff. But when someone leaves a big heart taped to Sludge's doghouse, Nate must help his favorite pooch discover his secret admirer.

- **Nate the Great and the Tardy Tortoise:** Where did the mysterious green tortoise in Nate's yard come from? Nate needs all his patience to follow this slow . . . slow . . . clue.

- **Nate the Great and the Crunchy Christmas:** It's Christmas, and Fang, Annie's scary dog, is not feeling jolly. Can Nate find Fang's crunchy Christmas mail before Fang crunches on *him*?

- **Nate the Great Saves the King of Sweden:** Can Nate solve his *first-ever* international case without leaving his own neighborhood?

- **Nate the Great and Me: The Case of the Fleeing Fang:** A surprise Happy Detective Day party is great fun for Nate until his friend's dog disappears! Help Nate track down the missing pooch, and learn all the tricks of the trade in a special fun section for aspiring detectives.

❏ **Nate the Great and the Monster Mess:** Nate loves his mother's deliciously spooky Monster Cookies, but the recipe has vanished! This is one case Nate and his growling stomach can't afford to lose.

❏ **Nate the Great, San Francisco Detective:** Nate visits his cousin Olivia Sharp in the big city, but it's no vacation. Can he find a lost joke book in time to save the world?

❏ **Nate the Great and the Big Sniff:** Nate depends on his dog, Sludge, to help him solve all his cases. But Nate is on his own this time, because Sludge has disappeared! Can Nate solve the case and recover his canine buddy?

❏ **Nate the Great on the Owl Express:** Nate boards a train to guard Hoot, his cousin Olivia Sharp's pet owl. Then Hoot vanishes! Can Nate find out *whooo* took the feathered creature?

❏ **Nate the Great Talks Turkey:** There's a turkey on the loose, with Nate, his cousin Olivia Sharp, Sludge, and Claude in hot pursuit. Who will find the runaway bird first?

❏ **Nate the Great and the Hungry Book Club:** Rosamond has started a book club. Nate and his dog, Sludge, attend a meeting as undercover detectives. The case: find out what "monster" has an appetite for ripping book pages and making others go missing.